# Here Come the Purim Players!

Barbara Cohen
Illustrated by Shoshana Mekibel

UAHC Press
New York, New York

"They're coming! They're coming!
The Purim players are coming!"

All the Jews who lived in the Prague ghetto lined the narrow streets, shouting, cheering, and laughing so hard that tears ran down their cheeks. The only ones who weren't there were buried six feet under the ground in the old graveyard.

Reb Yisroel led the way, riding his black horse. Mottel was a clown, with a red veil over his head, like a woman, and Moishe was another clown, pots and pans hanging by strings from the folds of his cloak. The boys from the yeshiva pulled the wine cask. Chaim Yankel sat on top of it, like a king.

Reb Yisroel dismounted from his mare and tied her to the hitching post in front of Reb Zalman's house. With his long, beribboned staff, he knocked on Reb Zalman's door. Shayne Sarah, Reb Zalman's daughter, opened the door, and all the Purim players trooped inside.

The crowd in the street surged in behind them until Reb Zalman's dining room was packed with as many people as it could hold. And those who couldn't fit inside peered through the open windows. Little Rifka climbed on her father's shoulders. Tsine pushed her head under her husband Yakov's arm. And those who couldn't see had to be content to listen.

Reb Yisroel introduced the play. "Long ago," he announced, "many Jews lived in Shushan, the capital of Persia. The ruler of all the Medes and all the Persians was King Ahasuerus."

Shayne Sarah's betrothed, red-headed Nachum, leaped forward and bowed to the audience. He was to play the king.

"Now, King Ahasuerus had a wife," said Reb Yisroel. "Her name was Queen Vashti. And he had a powerful adviser, too, whom he trusted completely. His name was…"

"*Haman!*" shouted all the people in Reb Zalman's dining room as they booed and hissed and stamped their feet. Chaim Yankel banged on the wine cask with an iron soup ladle, and Yussele plucked the strings of the bass fiddle in the corner. Pavel the fishmonger nodded coldly, his nose wrinkled in a sneer. He was playing Haman.

"In Shushan it so happened that there lived a Jew named Mordecai," Reb Yisroel continued. "With your kind permission, I will undertake that role. And if you will further honor us with your patience and indulgence, young Anshel here will impersonate the beautiful orphan Esther, who lives with her cousin Mordecai."

"Hooray for Mordecai," shouted the crowd. "Hooray for Esther."

"A party," cried red-headed Nachum, playing the part of King Ahasuerus. "I'm having a great banquet for all the noblemen in my kingdom." He picked up a glass of wine from the table and swallowed it down in one gulp. Mottel and Moishe and Chaim Yankel instantly threw back their heads and poured wine down their own throats, too.

"Look, Papa," said Rifka, "they're drunk."

"Not really drunk," replied Rifka's papa. "Just pretending."

Haman bowed before Ahasuerus. "O mighty king, send for your wife," he cried. "Order Queen Vashti to come here and entertain us."

King Ahasuerus sent for Vashti. But Vashti was a queen, not an entertainer. She sent back a message: "I will not come."

As if they were one person, the audience gasped.

"She won't come?" Haman exploded. "She won't come? What a terrible example to set for all the wives of the kingdom. O my lord, you will have to punish her."

King Ahasuerus sent Vashti away from Shushan. Now he needed a new queen. "A new queen. Where will I find a new queen?" he asked.

"A contest," Tsine's husband Yakov called out. "You should hold a contest."

"Good idea!" Ahasuerus exclaimed. "I will hold a contest."

Mordecai told Esther about the contest. "You will have to appear before the king," he said. "All the young girls in Persia must go."

"No," said Esther. "I don't want to go. I want to stay here with you."

"You must go," Mordecai told her. "The chances are that the king won't choose you. Then you will come home again, and nothing will have changed. But if he does choose you, it will be for a reason."

So Esther went to the palace of King Ahasuerus. Gold robes, jewelry studded with gems, perfumes, rouges, and powders were laid out in a great hall. Each girl could choose what she wanted to make herself perfect for the king.

Esther didn't want to be queen. She didn't want to change herself. She went before the king in a plain white dress.

Esther chose nothing. But the king said, "I choose Esther."

On hearing those three words, "I choose Esther," the Jews of Prague cheered and clapped their hands.

King Ahasuerus loved Queen Esther. He didn't know she was a Jew.

The king didn't know Haman was wicked, either. Haman ordered every person he met to bow down before him, as if he were the king himself. When Haman passed Mordecai in the courtyard, Mordecai stood straight as a cedar tree.

"How dare you?" cried Haman. "Bow this instant!"

"I am a Jew," Mordecai replied. "I bow only to God."

One night the king couldn't sleep. He ordered his scribe to read to him from the book in which was written everything that happened in the court.

"Bigthan and Teresh plotted to kill the king," the scribe intoned. "The Jew Mordecai overheard their evil plans and revealed them to the guards. Bigthan and Teresh were imprisoned and the king's life was saved."

"I never heard about this," said King Ahasuerus. "What was Mordecai's reward for such a noble deed?"

"None," replied the scribe. "No reward is recorded here."

The next day the king called Haman to him. "How should the king reward a man who deserves to be honored?"

Haman grinned at the audience. "It's me the king wishes to honor."

"That's what you think," Shayne Sarah called out from the audience. "That's what you think."

Haman bowed low before the king. "Dress the man in your own clothes," he said. "Mount him on your own horse. Have the greatest prince in the kingdom lead the horse through the streets of the city, crying, 'Behold the man the king wishes to honor.'"

"Very good," cried the king. "In just that way you will lead Mordecai the Jew through Shushan."

Haman's face turned purple. He did as the king ordered. He had no choice. But he vowed revenge.

Once more he came before the king. He bowed low. Then he whispered in the king's ear. "There is a certain people, living right here in your country, who have their own laws and their own gods. They could be traitors. Let me get rid of them for you."

King Ahasuerus waved his hand. "I can't be bothered with these trivial matters. Take my signet ring. Do what you want."

Haman issued an edict over the king's seal. On the fourteenth day of the month of Adar all the Jews in Persia were to be killed.

The audience inside and outside Reb Zalman's house sighed and groaned.

In Shushan's main courtyard Haman built a huge gallows. That was for Mordecai.

The audience inside and outside Reb Zalman's house sighed and groaned again. "Esther will save us," Rifka exclaimed. "Save us, Queen Esther!"

Mordecai went to see Esther in her own private palace. "Haman plans to kill all the Jews," he told her. "You must find a way to save us."

"I can't go before the king unless he sends for me," Esther protested. "Anyone who appears before the king without permission can be put to death. Even the queen. That's the law of this land."

Mordecai stared at Esther for a long time.

"I'll think about it," she said.

For one whole day Esther prayed and fasted.

Then she put on her most beautiful clothes. She walked down long corridors and across wide courtyards until she came to the palace of the king. She entered the throne room and threw herself at the king's feet.

"Oh, how brave she is!" whispered little Rifka.

The king held out his sceptre. Queen Esther's life was spared.

"Arise, my queen," said King Ahasuerus. "What is it that you want? I will grant it to you, even if it is half my kingdom."

"My lord," said Queen Esther, "please, let me entertain you. Come to a banquet in my palace tomorrow evening. Bring the mighty Haman with you."

"With pleasure, my queen," replied King Ahasuerus.

"With pleasure, my queen," echoed Haman.

The next evening Queen Esther and her maidens served King Ahasuerus and Haman every kind of wonderful delicacy. They filled their wine cups with wine again and again and again. Then, as before, Queen Esther threw herself at the king's feet.

"What is it that you want, my queen?" said the king. "I will grant it to you, even if it is half my kingdom."

In Reb Zalman's dining room, the only sound was Queen Esther's voice.

"My life," she whispered. "Only my life."

"Your life?" cried King Ahasuerus. "Who dares to threaten the queen's life?"

Esther stood up. She stretched out her hand, her finger pointing at Haman. "Him!" she cried.

"I?" Haman exclaimed. "I? I have nothing but the deepest respect and admiration for the queen. Nothing, I might add, but love."

Esther turned to the king. "On the fourteenth day of the month of Adar, all the Jews in Persia are to be killed, by order of this… this… Haman. My lord, I am a Jew!"

The king exploded with fury. "You have tricked me, Haman. I have trusted you, and you have betrayed me."

Guards dragged Haman off to prison. The king could not take back the orders that had gone out over his seal. But he sent out a new order, giving the Jews the right to defend themselves against anyone who might attack them.

Mordecai led his people into battle. On the fourteenth day of Adar, the Jews of Persia defeated their enemies.

On the great gallows that he had intended for Mordecai, Haman was hanged. "And you, Mordecai," King Ahasuerus announced, "from now on, you shall be my chief adviser."

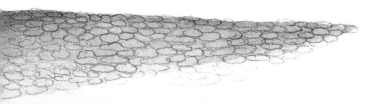

"Hooray, Mordecai!" shouted Rifka's papa.

"Hooray, Mordecai!" echoed every other person in the room, and every person outside, peering in.

Mordecai issued his first edict. "On the fourteenth day of Adar, all Jews will honor Queen Esther, who saved her people, with a joyful feast to be called Purim. On that day all Jews everywhere, now and forevermore, shall eat and drink and sing and dance and send charity to the poor."

Mordecai bowed low. Esther and King Ahasuerus and all the other players bowed low— even Haman.

The purim play was over. The players sang their last song.

Today is Purim,

Tomorrow—no more.

Give us a groschen

And show us the door.

Reb Zalman's servants carried trays of raisins, honey pastries, poppy seed cakes, brandy, and wine through the cheering, laughing, pushing crowd. Reb Zalman himself gave the players a handful of pennies. They danced out of the houses, still singing their song.

For a long time their music echoed among the wooden houses whose roofs seemed almost to touch in the middle of the road. At last the sound died away.

The narrow streets of the Prague ghetto are empty now, and silent.

Cover and book design by Itzhack Shelomi

Manufactured in the United States of America
10 9 8 7 6 5 4 3 2 1